TO SOPHIE

HAPPY READING!

Mark Collins

Where Did Summer Go?

Story and Pictures by Mark C. Collins

Edited by Stacy Radil

For those who love the sand, surf, and sun!

A part of Bright Ideas Graphics

Where has Summer gone?
It's cold and it's gray.
I feel so blue when
Summer goes away.

Summer was lovely.
I miss my best friend.
All the fun things we did,
I didn't want to end.

Sunning and swimming
And looking for shells...

Up on the boardwalk-
The sights and the smells.

But now that's all over
As fast as it started.
And beach life feels empty
Since Summer departed.

I hear the waves crash
And a seagull screech.
Mom holds my hand
As we walk on the beach.

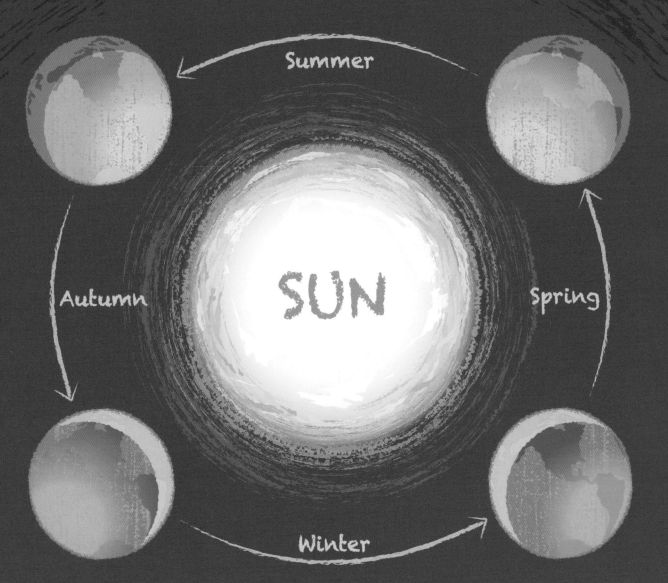

Mom says that Summer
Will come back next year.
But for now we allow
Old Man Winter to be here.

I look through the window
And out to the shore.
I just can't help thinking
Of Summer once more.

I finish my dinner
And take a hot bath.
Now time for my homework;
It's Science and Math!

I put on my apron
And help Mom bake bread,
While dreaming of Summer
And warm days ahead.

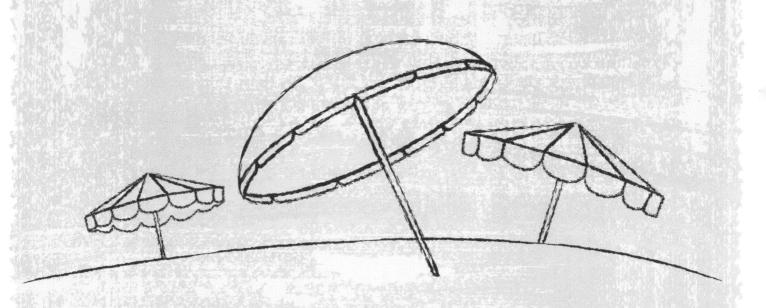

Winter has moved on.
We're now into Spring.
I can't wait to find out
What Summer will bring!

It's been a great school year
But I'm glad it's done.
I'm looking so forward
To sand, surf, and sun!

I hardly can wait for
The sunny, hot days
Of Summer's return
And playing in waves.

Today is the day!
We're well into June.
I sit back and wait
Atop a sand dune.

Look! There she is!
It's finally real.
Summer has come!
Can you guess how I feel?

We do all those fun things
That we did last year...

And rides on the pier.

I know she'll be leaving
By this season's end.
But for now, at this moment
It's just me and my friend.

The
End